The King of Quizzical Island

For dearest Maeve,
with all my love and thanks
on our wonderful journey
G. S.

For Aki and Satoru
D. M.

Text copyright © 1978, 2009 by Gordon Snell
Illustrations copyright © 1978, 2009 by David McKee

First U.S. edition 2009

Library of Congress Cataloging-in-Publication Data

Snell, Gordon.
The King of Quizzical Island / Gordon Snell ; illustrated by David McKee.
—1st ed.
p.   cm.
Summary: When no one can answer his question about what is
at the edge of the world, the King of Quizzical Island builds a
boat and sets sail to find out for himself, despite the objections
of his fearful people.
ISBN 978-0-7636-3857-3
[1. Explorers—Fiction. 2. Voyages and travels—Fiction.
3. Kings, queens, rulers, etc.—Fiction.
4. Questions and answers—Fiction. 5. Earth—Fiction.]
I. McKee, David, ill. II. Title.
PZ8.3.S6725Kin 2010
[E]—dc22   2008026510

1 2 3 4 5 6 7 8 9 10

Printed in China

This book was typeset in Avenir.
The illustrations were done in pen, ink, and watercolor.

Candlewick Press
99 Dover Street
Somerville, Massachusetts 02144

visit us at www.candlewick.com

The King of Quizzical Island

Gordon Snell

illustrated by

David McKee

CANDLEWICK PRESS

The King of Quizzical Island
Had a most inquisitive mind.

He said, "If I sail to the edge of the world,

I wonder what I'll find."

He quizzed his wily old Wizard

And the Whispering Witches, too—

The Llama, the Leopard, the Lizard,

And the Owl—but none of them knew.

So the King of Quizzical Island

Made up his inquisitive mind,

And he said, "I'll sail to the edge of the world

And find . . . what I shall find."

———————————————————

"I'll build myself a singular ship

Made of wood from the Tea-Bag Tree,

And I'll sail that ship to the edge of the world

And see . . . what I shall see."

His fearful people pleaded.

They wept fat tears of woe.

Some said, "Remain!" and some, "Please stay!"

While others said, "Don't go!"

"For it's quite well known, and I've heard it said

By wise men, old and clever,

That those who sail to the edge of the world

Fall off—and fall forever."

———————————————————————

But the King of Quizzical Island

Said, "Tosh!" and "Bosh!" and "Twaddle!"

"For I can sail to the edge of the world

As sure as a duck can waddle."

So he built himself a singular ship

Made of wood from the Tea-Bag Tree,

And the rigging was a spider's web

And the rudder a bumblebee.

The ship sailed out of the harbor

And its silken sails unfurled

As the King of Quizzical Island

Set sail for the edge of the world.

He sailed through waves as high as hills

For thirty days or more

Until at last, the ship was cast

On a higgledy-piggledy shore.

He found himself in a Jigsaw Land,

Which lay there, all in pieces:

The blue bits might have been sea, or sky,

Or sheep with ink-stained fleeces.

The green bits might have been grass, or leaves,

Or a snake or a dragon's tail,

And the white bits might have been clouds, or snow,

Or the teeth of a smiling whale.

It took the king nine days and nights

To fit those bits in place.

Then he saw before him a river,

And a smile lit up his face.

So he sailed up that Jigsaw River,

And there, round the final bend,

He found himself in Vertical Land,

Where everything stands on end.

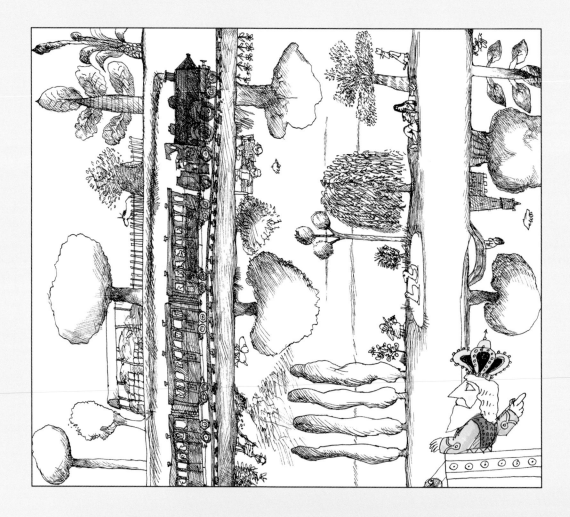

The rivers go up like fountains

And the crocodiles stand on their tails

And the meadows tower like mountains

And the trains run on vertical rails.

The king said, "That's *one* way of using

Every inch of space you've got,

But it doesn't look very comfortable."

And the crocodiles said, "It's not!"

So the singular ship sailed upward

On a river tall and wide,

And from the top of the river

It sailed down the other side.

It sailed through Hurricane Harriet

To the Sea of Dreadful Dreams,

Where the waves are forever wailing

And the Wild Wind sighs and screams,

Where the Sea Horse turns into a Night Mare

And prances upon the foam,

And gaggles of ghostly jellyfish

Wobble their way back home.

"All things ghastly and ghoulish,"
Said the king, "I can put to flight.
They'll all feel extremely foolish
When I wake and turn on the light."

He rang a hundred alarm clocks,

And the Sky switched on the Sun,

And the Dreadful Dreams were ended

As quickly as they'd begun.

The wild wind sank to a whisper

And even the waves were shy

And the moon smiled down, benignly,

From the sleeping deeps of the sky.

The King of Quizzical Island

Sailed on, till he sighted land.

And the singular ship was beached upon

A handy, sandy strand.

He looked at the castle before him,

And knew he had seen it before,

And he said, "I've sailed to the edge of the world

And arrived at my own backdoor!"

His people rushed out to greet him;

They gave him a rousing cheer.

And he said, "There is no edge of the world.

The world is a perfect sphere.

"I sailed out there in my singular ship,

And I'll tell you what I found.

I found I was back at my own backdoor—

So I've proved that the world is round!"

Everyone cheered and shouted;

They shouted and cheered and kissed.

Their king had come back from the edge of the world

And proved it didn't exist!

Only the Owl was doubtful.

He said, "If the earth is flat,

You *might* have sailed round in a circle

And arrived where you started at."

The King of Quizzical Island

Was more than a bit put out.

He said, "Nonsense!" and "Bosh" and "Balderdash!"

But he still had a lingering doubt.

He said, "In Quizzical Island,

Answers must always be found,

And I have another perilous plan

To prove that the world is round.

"I shall build myself a singular spade,

Made of diamonds, ten feet wide,

And I'll dig a tunnel, far into the world,

And come out at the other side!"

The people, they gasped in wonder.

They said, "Gosh!" and "Gulp!" and "Glory!"
As the king began digging into the world . . .

But that is another story.

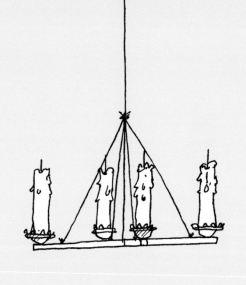